Look What Brown Can Do!

First Edition
Author: Harris, T. Marie
Title: Look What Brown Can Do!
Target Audience: For primary school age
ISBN-13: 978-0692483862 (Pbk.)
ISBN-10: 0692483861

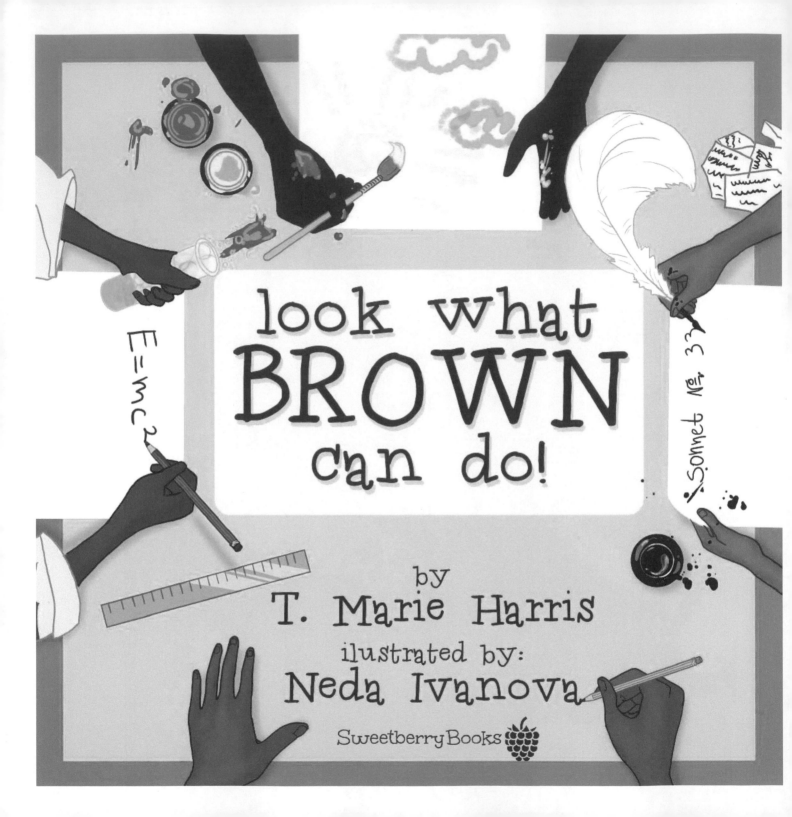

look what BROWN can do!

$E=mc^2$

Sonnet № 33

by
T. Marie Harris

illustrated by:
Neda Ivanova

Sweetberry Books

To Dearest & Papa,

Thank you
for showing us exactly how much Brown can do.

Look what BROWN can do!

Brown can inspire through art ...
and I CAN TOO!

Gordon Parks

Brown can become one of the most celebrated photojournalists in the U.S. as well as the first Black to write, direct, and score a Hollywood film.

Meta Vaux Warrick Fuller

Brown can become one of the most imaginative Black artists of her generation as the first Black female sculptor of importance.

Palmer Hayden

Brown can pursue his passion for over 30 years before becoming a renown painter who contributed to the artistic community well into his 80's.

Look what BROWN can do!
Brown can be a business success ...
and I CAN TOO!

Robert L. Johnson

Brown can become the first Black billionaire by creating the first cable television network aimed at Black Americans (BET), then later become the first Black majority owner of a major American sports league.

Janice Bryant Howroyd

Brown can start her own business, grow it into a global operation and become the first Black woman to own a billion dollar company.

Reginald F. Lewis

Brown can become a successful investor at his own venture capital firm, leading him to be the first Black American to own and build a billion dollar company.

Look what BROWN can do!
Brown can move the world through music ...
and I CAN TOO!

Wynton Marsalis

Brown can win 9 Grammy Awards and become the only artist to win Grammys in both Jazz and Classical genres; then go on to become the first musician ever to win the Pulitzer Prize for Music.

Kazem Abdullah

Brown can become one of the most watched conductors on the international stage, listed as one of the top 5 "Young Rock Stars of the Conducting World."

Leontyne Price

Brown can become the first Black American to sing lead at the Metropolitan Opera and the first Black American to gain international acclaim as a professional opera singer, winning 19 Grammy Awards; more than any other classical singer.

Look what BROWN can do!
Brown can lead in government ...
and I CAN TOO!

President Barack Obama

Brown can be elected as the first Black American editor of the Harvard Law Review, elected to the U.S. Senate with the largest electoral victory in Illinois history, and become the first Black American president of the United States.

AG Loretta Lynch

Brown can become the first Black American female to hold the office of United States Attorney General.

President Ellen Johnson Sirleaf

Brown can become the world's first elected Black female president and Africa's first female elected head of state, then later become the recipient of the Nobel Peace Prize.

Look what BROWN can do!

Brown can change the world of medicine ...

and I CAN TOO!

Dr. Daniel Hale Williams

Brown can open the first hospital to employ and serve Black and White patients side by side; and become the first surgeon to successfully perform open heart surgery.

Percy Julian, PhD

Brown can become the first Black to earn a PhD in Chemistry and make an important discovery that becomes the foundation for medicine doctors use all over the world.

Dr. Alexa Canady

Brown can become the first Black female doctor to treat the brain, spine, and peripheral nerves (neurosurgeon), and help invent an important device that treats fluid in the brain.

Look what BROWN can do!
Brown can express through The Arts ...
and I CAN TOO!

August Wilson

Brown can become a self-taught, two-time Pulitzer Prize and Tony Award winning playwright, and be the recipient of the first Broadway theatre to be named after a Black American.

Dr. Maya Angelou

Brown can become an internationally acclaimed author, poet, actress and singer, and make literary history as the first Black American woman to write a non-fiction bestseller

Misty Copeland

Brown can become one of the first Black dancers to play the leading role in a top company's production of Swan Lake, and be the first Black American female soloist in 20 years at the American Ballet Theatre.

Look what BROWN can do!
Brown can invent to change the world ...
and I CAN TOO!

Jesse Russell

Brown can become one of the key pioneers to the invention of the modern cell phone by creating over 75 inventions in digital cellular technologies, dual-mode digital cellular phones, and digital software radio.

Marie Van Brittan Brown

Brown can change the home security market as we know it today by inventing the first camera monitored home security system.

Frederick McKinley Jones

Brown can create over 60 world changing inventions; including a portable air conditioner for trucks carrying food, a portable x-ray machine, sound equipment, and gasoline engines.

Look what BROWN can do!
Brown can be an all star athlete ...
and I CAN TOO!

Vincent "Bo" Jackson

Brown can have a successful career in both MLB and the NFL, and become the only athlete named All-Star in two major American sports.

Pelé

Brown can become one of the best professional soccer players to ever play the game, winning 3 World Cups and scoring more competition points than any other player.

Althea Gibson

Brown can become the first Black player to compete on the women's professional golf tour, the first Black athlete to play international tennis, and the first person of color to win a Grand Slam title at the French Open.

Little BROWN

We're so proud of you!

When you grow up, what might you do?

I Can Too!

About The

About The

AUTHOR

T. Marie Harris is an early childhood educator with a passion for storytelling. After leaving a successful career in pharmaceutical sales to pursue her dream of educating, T. Marie joined Teach For America Corps 2011 and began teaching elementary school in Washington D.C.

Here she noticed a glaring disparity of Black characters and titles presented in literary works, but it wasn't until she had her own children and found it increasingly difficult to find books highlighting Black characters, that she decided to create a line of books of her own.

"Look What Brown Can Do!" is the first in the 'Brown Like Me' series that features early reader books with an array of beautiful Black characters. The 'Brown Like Me' series uniquely includes titles centered around the joys of being Black, as well as everyday fun, entertaining, stories featuring Black characters without focus on race. Sometimes it's just nice to read a story with characters that look like your children, and students.

T. Marie Harris is an HBCU alumna and former Miss Bethune-Cookman College. She lives in Northern Virginia with her husband and two young children.

 @T_MarieHarris

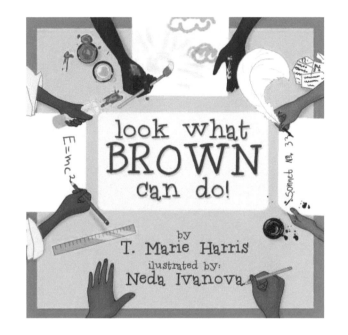

Additional copies may be obtained from
Amazon.com or directly through

www.lookwhatbrowncando.com

CPSIA information can be obtained
at www.ICGtesting.com
Printed in the USA
LVHW071203200620
658571LV00030B/1488